9/91

JN

Merry Christmas,
AMANDA & APRIL

Merry Christmas,
AMANDA & APRIL

Bonnie Pryor

Illustrated by Diane de Groat

Morrow Junior Books

New York

Printed in Singapore at Tien Wah Press.
1 2 3 4 5 6 7 8 9 10
Library of Congress Cataloging-in-Publication Data
Pryor, Bonnie.
Merry Christmas, Amanda & April / Bonnie Pryor : illustrated by
Diane de Groat.
p.   cm.
Summary: Trying her best to be good before Christmas, Amanda Pig
does an errand for her mother and is helped by her little sister, April.
ISBN 0-688-07544-4—ISBN 0-688-07545-2 (lib. bdg.)
[1. Pigs—Fiction. 2. Sisters—Fiction. 3. Christmas—Fiction.]
I. De Groat, Diane, ill.   II. Title: Merry Christmas,
Amanda and April.
PZ7.P94965Me   1990
[E]—dc20   89-39723   CIP   AC

To Tabitha, who's brand-new

B.P.

"I'm bored," said Amanda. She looked out the window just in time to see Violet Skunk walk by in a brand-new pair of snowshoes.

"You have to stay inside until your cold is better," said her sister, April.

"I haven't had one sniffle all day," Amanda answered crossly.

Mrs. Pig felt Amanda's head. "I think you are well enough to go to the store. I need a few things to make a surprise for Santa."

"Hurray!" Amanda said happily. She hoped Santa would see her helping Mama. Amanda wanted a Snuggly Baby Pig for Christmas, with a curly tail and a voice that said "Mama" when you pulled a string. But she wasn't sure she had been good enough for such a wonderful present.

"All right," said Mrs. Pig. "Put on your coat and boots. And wear your new hat so your ears don't get cold. I want you to go straight to the store and come back. Then we will make the surprise for Santa."

"May I go, too?" asked April.

"Of course," said Mrs. Pig. "Amanda, help April put on her coat and snowpants."

This did not make Amanda happy. April did not need to show Santa how good she was. April was always good. Amanda took April's hat and hid it in the back of the closet behind Mama's old pocketbook.

"I guess you can't go," she told April. "I can't find your hat."

April started to cry, and Amanda peeked out the window. Maybe Santa was watching right now. "Here is your hat," she said quickly. "You can go, after all."

Mrs. Pig handed Amanda a list and a purseful of money.
"I need butter and eggs and flour," she said. But Amanda
was not really listening. She was too busy thinking about
going outdoors.

Amanda and April walked down the road. The snow on
the trees sparkled in the sun. "Let's make snow angels," said
April.

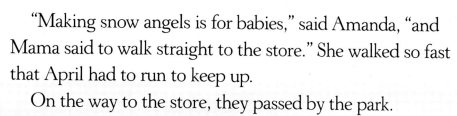

"Making snow angels is for babies," said Amanda, "and Mama said to walk straight to the store." She walked so fast that April had to run to keep up.

On the way to the store, they passed by the park. Amanda stopped to watch the children playing in the snow. Some were making snowmen, and others were sledding down the hill. All of them were having fun.

"The store is on the other side of the park," said Amanda.

April shook her head. "I don't think Mama wants us to go into the park."

"We are not going to play," Amanda explained. "We'll walk straight across the park, just like Mama said."

"Come and slide down the hill," called Amanda's friend Henrietta.

"I am sure Mama won't mind if I take one tiny ride," Amanda said to April. "I'll be careful not to fall in the snow."

April waited while Amanda and Henrietta pulled the sled to the top of the hill. She made five snow angels and a Grandfather Pig with a curly tail. Amanda zoomed down the hill again and again.

Barney and Clyde were sledding down Monster Hill.

"Watch out," shouted Clyde. "This hill is much too high for babies."

"Ha," said Amanda with a sniff. "I slide down bigger hills than that all the time."

"Prove it," said Barney.

Amanda looked up Monster Hill. It was so big that it almost touched the sky. But she did not want Barney and Clyde to think she was a baby.

Then she remembered something. "I don't have a sled," said Amanda. "I will have to show you another day."

"You can use one of our sleds," said Clyde.
Amanda pulled the sled up Monster Hill. She could see
April far below. April looked very worried.

Amanda waved at April but just then her foot slipped in the icy snow. She went whooshing down the hill faster and faster until she reached the bottom and crashed into a tree.

Amanda stood up and brushed off the snow. She felt awful. She was cold, and she could feel a great big bump on her elbow.

"Look," said April. Billy Goat was throwing snowballs at old Mrs. Hound.

"Stop that!" Amanda yelled.

"You'd better watch out," called Barney and Clyde. "Amanda is so tough she can slide down Monster Hill without using a sled."

Billy threw one last snowball and ran away. Mrs. Hound looked so cold and unhappy that Amanda gave her the new hat.

Mrs. Hound pulled the hat over her ears. "Oh, thank you," she said. Then Amanda wished her a merry Christmas and waved good-bye as the sisters hurried on to the store.

* *

Amanda looked in her pocket for the list, but it was gone. "Don't worry," she said when April frowned. "I know we are out of ice cream. That was probably one of the things on Mama's list."

April shook her head. "Mama did not say to buy ice cream. She said to buy butter and eggs and something else...."

"Butter and eggs are boring," said Amanda, putting them in the basket. She picked up a bag of chocolate-covered gumdrops. "Maybe these were on the list. I'm sure they are Santa's favorite treat."

April put the gumdrops back on the shelf. She was thinking hard. "Mama did not say to buy candy," she said to Amanda. "She said to buy flowers."

"Flowers?" asked Amanda. "Why would Mama want flowers?"

"Maybe they're part of Santa's surprise," April said. "There aren't any flowers at the North Pole."

They chose a beautiful bunch of daisies for Santa. Then they stood in line to pay Mr. Hog.

FLOWER SALE

"How much is this bag of flour?" Mrs. Skunk was asking Mr. Hog.

"Uh-oh," said April. "Did Mama tell us to buy flowers or flour?"

Amanda counted out the money. "We have enough for both," she said happily. "That must be what Mama meant."

It was almost dark when Amanda and April arrived home. Mrs. Pig was waiting by the door and she looked cross. "You were supposed to go straight to the store," she said. "And, Amanda, where is your hat?"

April told Mrs. Pig about sliding down Monster Hill and rescuing old Mrs. Hound.

"Don't be mad, Mama," Amanda said quickly. "Mrs. Hound looked very cold. I don't mind wearing my old hat." She held her breath until Mama began to smile.

"What a good pig you are," said Mama. Then she looked in the bag. "What is this?"

"We got flour and flowers," Amanda answered. "Just like you said."

Mama looked very surprised, but she smiled. "We will use the flour to make cookies for Santa. And I will put these pretty flowers in a vase."

Amanda and April helped Mama make the cookies. They ate quite a few, but there was still a big plateful for Santa. Amanda placed it right beside the tree, next to the daisies. "I wonder which one Santa will like best," she said.

When Santa came that night, he was pleased to see his gifts. "Ho, ho, ho," Santa laughed. He ate three cookies and stuck a daisy in his hat. Then he wrote a note and left it by two Snuggly Baby Pigs that said "Mama" when you pulled a string.

Dear Amanda and April,
I liked both of my gifts. I hope you like yours.
Love, Santa

And they did.